Published by Grolier Incorporated, 90 Old Sherman Turnpike, Danbury,
Connecticut 06816, a subsidiary of Scholastic Inc.,
by arrangement with Disney Enterprises, Inc.

ISBN 0-7172-6545-5

10 9 8 7 6 5 4 3 2 1   01 02 03 04 05

Printed in the U.S.A.
First printing, October 2001

GROLIER
B O O K S

DISNEP's
MICKEY & MINNIE'S
GIFT OF THE MAGI

by Bruce Talkington

Illustrated by Fernando Guell Cano

It was the day before Christmas. The bright morning
sun was sparkling on the freshly fallen snow. There was a
chill in the air as Mickey and Pluto strolled down the street.

Mickey's coat was not warm enough. His Christmas tree was not large enough. And his pockets were as empty as the stockings soon to be hung in homes all over town. But Mickey happily played music on his harmonica.

Suddenly Pluto started to bark. He pulled Mickey
by his sleeve over to a shop window. In the window
was a beautiful gold necklace. It twinkled in the
morning sunlight.

"There it is Pluto," sighed Mickey. "The perfect
gift to go with Minnie's watch."

Mickey reached into his empty pockets.
"Well, I'm a little short right now. But, uh,
you and I are going to make lots of tips today,
aren't we, fella?" said Mickey hopefully.

Pluto looked doubtful.

Mickey told him they would come back
and buy the necklace later. "Come on," said
Mickey, "let's get this tree over to Minnie's."

Meanwhile, at her home, Minnie worried over a pile of unpaid bills. "Oh, Figaro," she sighed to her cat. Figaro purred sadly. "There's nothing but bills. How am I ever going to afford to get Mickey a present?"

Just then Minnie's front door opened. It was Mickey! Minnie quickly shoved the bills in a drawer and raced into the living room.

There was Mickey, playing a happy song on his harmonica and carrying a tree.

Minnie gazed at him and giggled. "Ah, Mickey, when you play the harmonica my heart sings."

Mickey brought the tree inside. Then he began
to wrap his harmonica in an old rag. "You know an
instrument like that deserves a special case,"
Minnie told him.

"Oh, yeah," sighed Mickey, "someday."

Mickey pretended not to see the clock on the wall and asked Minnie what time it was.

"Let's see," Minnie replied, pulling a string out of her pocket. On the end of the string hung a lovely old watch.

"That sure is a beautiful watch," said Mickey.

"My one heirloom," Minnie said proudly.

"I'll bet it'd look real nice on a gold chain around your pretty neck," Mickey commented.

Suddenly Minnie took another look at her watch. "Oh, my goodness!" she cried. "I've got to go to work!" She quickly put her watch away and headed to the door.

But Mickey beat her outside. He and Pluto wanted to drop Minnie off at work—in style!

"Oh, how wonderful!" Minnie gushed.

After a wild ride, Pluto pulled up
in front of Mortimer's Department
Store, just in time for Minnie's work.

Minnie hopped off and gave Mickey a quick kiss. As she headed in for work she called, "See you tonight!"

Mickey watched her go. Then he said to Pluto, "Come on, fella, we have work to do!" and they hurried off.

Unfortunately, Mickey arrived late for work at Crazy Pete's Christmas Tree Farm. "Merry Christmas, Mr. Crazy Pete," Mickey tried to say.

"Merry shmerry," grumbled Pete. "I'll be merry when I've sold all those ten footers," he said, pointing at some trees. "Get to work!"

The day turned out to be better
than Mickey expected—
despite Crazy Pete.
Customers were so happy
with Mickey's help with
their trees that he earned
a lot of extra money.

"Hot dog!" Mickey exclaimed.
"Looks like we'll finally be able to get Minnie
that chain for her watch!" he told Pluto.

Nearby, Pete was trying to convince a poor father to buy a huge, expensive Christmas tree for his children. "This is all I got left," Pete lied. "You don't want these kids going without a tree now, do ya?"

Mickey overheard what was happening and didn't think Pete was being fair. "Hey, how about this tree?" called Mickey. "I found it out back."

"It's perfect!" cried the children.

"We'll take it!" cried the father. "Thank you! Merry Christmas!"

Pete was furious. "I had them on the hook for a ten-foot tree!" he growled at Mickey. "I'm taking what I would have made off that tree outta *your* pay!" Then he grabbed all of Mickey's money.

"But, but I—" began Mickey.

"NOW GET OUT OF MY SIGHT!" roared Pete, tossing Mickey and Pluto headfirst into the snow.

Pete laughed as Mickey and Pluto left. He thought he
had outsmarted them. But he didn't notice that he put his lit
cigar in the same pocket as the money. Before Pete knew it,
his clothes had caught fire! Then, Pete's Christmas trees
caught fire.

When the firefighters arrived, Crazy Pete's Christmas Tree Farm was up in flames!

At Mortimer's, Minnie had wrapped many more
Christmas gifts than usual that day.

"Who made you Santa's number-one helper?" Daisy
joked to Minnie.

"I really want to get Mickey something special this
year," Minnie explained. "Without that Christmas bonus,
I'm sunk." Suddenly the phone rang. Daisy answered it.
It was the boss, asking Minnie to come to his office!

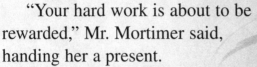

"Your hard work is about to be rewarded," Mr. Mortimer said, handing her a present.

"A fruitcake?" Minnie exclaimed, surprised. She tried to hide her disappointment.

"No need to thank me," replied Mr. Mortimer. "Now scoot along!"

Minnie left Mr. Mortimer's office. "Oh, Mickey," she sighed. "How am I ever going to get your present now?"

Meanwhile, Mickey sat in the park and played his harmonica. He had lost his job *and* his money. How could he pay for Minnie's present now? He hoped his music might spark an idea. Pluto sadly howled along.

But Pete had ruined more than just *Mickey's* Christmas this year. The firefighters' band had been playing music to raise toys for the local orphans for Christmas. Pete's burning trees had taken them away from that fundraiser. All seemed lost—until suddenly someone heard Mickey's harmonica!

The people in charge of the toy drive asked
Mickey if he'd play for the crowd until the band
came back. Mickey quickly accepted. Soon
Mickey's music was delighting everyone.

When the firefighters returned, they found that Mickey had saved the day. The crowd had donated lots of toys. In fact, the bin was filled to the top! The local orphans were going to have a wonderful Christmas after all!

Mickey continued to play with the band and had a great time.

"You and that harmonica sure make a great team," the fire chief told Mickey.

"Yup," agreed Mickey. "She's worth her weight in gold all right." Suddenly Mickey's eyes lit up. "Holy cow! That's it!" He looked at the clock. "We've still got two minutes to get to the shop. Come on, Pluto!"

The pair took off through the town. They even borrowed a snowboard and *whooshed* through the streets to get there in time.

Mickey and Pluto made it to the
shop just as the shopkeeper was
locking the door.

But he was too late! Mickey sat on the curb and played a sad tune on his harmonica.

Touched by the melody, the shopkeeper changed his mind about closing his shop. He agreed to let Mickey trade his harmonica for the gold necklace in the window.

Later that night, Mickey and Minnie sat in front of the fire. Pluto and Figaro watched excitedly.

"Uh, isn't it time we were opening our presents?" asked Mickey.

Minnie unwrapped her gift. "Oh, my, a chain for my watch!" she exclaimed. "Mickey, it's beautiful." But Minnie had traded her watch to get Mickey his present.

Mickey unwrapped his gift. "A case . . . heh, heh, for my harmonica," he said. "I traded my harmonica to get a chain for your watch!" Mickey confessed.

"Oh, Mickey, I can't believe you gave up what means the most to you *for me*," cooed Minnie.

"Oh, Minnie, you're all the music I'll ever need," Mickey told her.

"Merry Christmas, Mickey," said Minnie.
Mickey took her hand. "Merry Christmas."
And the couple was as content
as Pluto and Figaro who were
curled up on the floor. It was a
Christmas they'd never forget.